Apples

Helen Dunmore

illustrated by Simone Lia

Also in the **MAMMOTH STORYBOOK** series:

Magic Betsey Malorie Blackman
Blair the Winner! Theresa Breslin
Tricky Tricky Twins Kate Elizabeth Ernest
Pest Friends Pippa Goodhart
Little Mouse Grandma Julia Jarman
Hot Dog, Cool Cat Jenny Nimmo

First published in Great Britain in 1997
by Mammoth, an imprint of Reed International Books Ltd
Michelin House, 81 Fulham Road, London SW3 6RB
and Auckland, Melbourne, Singapore and Toronto

'Allie's Apples'
first published in 1995 in *Dear Mum, Don't Panic!*,
edited by Tony Bradman

Text copyright © 1995, 1997 Helen Dunmore
Illustrations copyright © 1997 Simone Lia

The rights of Helen Dunmore and Simone Lia to be identified as the
author and illustrator of this work have been asserted by them in
accordance with the Copyright, Designs and Patents Act 1988

ISBN 0 7497 2831 0

10 9 8 7 6 5 4 3 2 1

A CIP catalogue record for this book
is available from the British Library

Printed in Great Britain by Cox & Wyman Ltd,
Reading, Berkshire

Contents

~

For Tess
H.D.

For my mum & dad
S.L.

1

Allie's apples

'You can't fit a tree in our garden!' said Allie.

'Oh yes you can,' said Jacqueline in her big, sure voice. Allie looked round the garden. There was only just room for the climbing frame. Allie climbed to the top of the frame and swung her feet near Jacqueline's face.

'Oh no you can't,' she sang.

'Wait till Mum comes home, then you'll see,' said Jacqueline.

Why didn't Mum tell *me* about the

1

tree? thought Allie.

The doorbell rang. Allie peeped through the spyhole and saw a green waving thing instead of a person. Then she heard Mum's voice.

'Open the door quick, before I drop it!'

Allie flung the door open and a tree walked into the house. Behind it was Mum. She held the small tree in a round brown tub. It had smooth thin branches and bright leaves. Mum staggered into the hall and dumped the tub.

'Ooh, my back!' she said. 'I've carried that tub all the way from the garden centre.' But she was smiling.

'What's in it?' asked Allie, but Jacqueline pushed in front of her.

'It's an apple-tree, isn't it, Mum?' she said.

'You only know because you read the label,' said Allie.

It didn't look like an apple-tree. How could apples hang on those skinny branches? Then Mum showed Allie the buds.

'That's where the flowers are going to be,' she said, 'and when the flowers die, there'll be apples.'

Mum put the apple-tree tub in the corner of the garden where it would get the sun. There was just room for it.
Every night she watered it and sometimes she gave it plant food in the water. When Allie was in bed she peeped through her curtains and there was Mum, looking after her apple-tree.

'Mum,' Allie called through the window, 'come and read me a story!'

'No, Allie, you've had your story. Go to sleep. I've got to give this tree more water.'

'Mum likes that tree better than anything,' Allie whispered to Jacqueline, but Jacqueline was asleep.

Pink flowers came out on the tree, then died off into prickly brown lumps, which Mum said would grow into apples.

'I bet they won't,' said Allie, but Mum just smiled. Soon there were ten tiny hard little apples.

'Don't touch them,' warned Mum. 'They won't be ready till after the summer.' Allie snatched back her hand. 'If you touch the apples, Allie, they will fall off.'

After the summer! thought Allie.

Jacqueline will be ten by then.

One morning there were five small, hard, green apples on the concrete under the tub. They had fallen off in the night.

'It wasn't me! I didn't touch them!' said Allie.

'I know,' said Mum. 'Sometimes they drop off like that.'

'Only five left,' said Jacqueline bossily. 'I'll look after them for you, Mum.' And she gave Allie a hard look, as if Allie really had touched the apples.

But on Saturday, next-door's cat had a fight and came flying over the fence on top of the apple-tree. Allie heard him screech and ran out to see.

None of the branches were broken but two apples were knocked off.

'Never mind, Spangles,' said Allie, 'you didn't mean to do it,' and she cradled the cat till he felt better.

The three apples that were left on the tree grew fatter and fatter, but they were still green.

'Not ripe yet,' said Mum. 'Be careful and don't play near the tree, Allie. We'll have one each when they're ready.'

But one night the wind grew and howled, and the rain spattered against Allie's window. She looked out and saw the top of the big tree next door bending. It creaked and groaned as the wind hit it.

The next morning there were leaves all over the concrete, and two bruised apples, which were already turning brown. Allie took a bite out of one, but

she had to spit
it out.

'Never mind,' said
Mum, 'at least there's
one left on the tree.
As long as nobody touches it . . .'

The apple that was left held on tight to
its branch. It seemed to know it was the
only one. Soon it began to change
colour. Its green turned to yellow, and
little red streaks appeared on its side.
Every day it grew redder and redder.

'We'll give it another week,' said
Mum.

'And I'll pick it,'
said Jacqueline, 'I'm
the oldest. Don't
you touch it, Allie.'

Allie stared at the apple. She liked watching it. Sometimes she thought she could see it getting redder. It was going to be the best apple in the world. If Allie was that apple, she wouldn't want to be picked by Jacqueline.

Next day Mum was at work, and Jacqueline was watching TV with her friend, Yasmin. They did not want Allie.

Allie went out in the garden and stood near the tree. She knew she would not hurt it. Jacqueline always thought Allie wanted to break things and spoil them, but she didn't.

Allie reached up and touched the apple. It was warm and smooth. She put her hand under it and weighed it. It filled her hand, big and heavy. Its red skin glowed. Allie wanted that apple more than anything she had ever wanted. She thought of Jacqueline picking the apple because she was the oldest. She thought of Jaqueline giving Mum the apple, and Mum smiling at Jacqueline. Jacqueline always had to do everything.

Allie stroked the apple, then she pulled, just a little. Suddenly the dry stalk which joined the apple to the tree gave way. Allie had picked the apple.

She turned and there was Jacqueline with Yasmin. 'You'll get killed!' hissed Jacqueline in a snaky voice. Allie put her hands behind her back and hid the apple. Then she ran upstairs. Tied in a sock in her drawer she had a pound left from her birthday money.

She ran past Jacqueline out of the front door and down the street to the corner shop. Mrs Patel was knitting at the counter. Allie put her pound and the apple on the counter.

'Have you got any apples like this?' she panted.

Mrs Patel frowned. 'I am not sure,' she said. 'That is an unusual kind of apple. Let me look.'

She bent over her cardboard boxes of fruit and took out some apples. They were a flat, dull red, but they were the best she had.

'Maybe if I polish them,' said Allie.

'Here's a cloth,' said Mrs Patel, and she helped Allie polish the dull apples until they shone. But they still didn't look like Mum's apple.

'How many can I buy for a pound?' asked Allie. Mrs Patel weighed them. They were so big Allie could only have eight. She ran home with the apples in a

paper bag. There was just time to do it before Mum got back.

Allie found some black thread in the kitchen drawer, and cut nine pieces. She tied one to each stalk of the apples she had bought, and one to Mum's apple. Then, very carefully, she tied each apple to a branch until the tree was covered with apples.

Jacqueline and Yasmin watched and laughed at Allie behind their hands. But Allie thought the tree looked beautiful. Then she heard Mum's key in the front door.

She wanted to run and hide under her duvet but she stayed where she was.

Mum came out into the garden with a tired face and two bags of shopping. She stood quite still when she saw the tree. Allie ran to her and hid her face against

Mum. She felt Mum begin to shake and she thought Mum was crying because her last apple had been picked. Then she heard the sounds Mum was making. She wasn't crying, she was laughing. She was looking at the tree of red apples and laughing.

'Two each, and one left over,' Mum said. 'Quick, get them off before they break the branches.'

Allie snipped the threads one by one. She laid each apple carefully on the concrete. Then she snipped the very last apple from the highest branch. It was rosy and warm and it smelled different from the shop apples. Allie held it tight in her hands for a second. She still wanted it more than anything she had ever wanted. Then Allie gave Mum her apple, and Mum smiled.

2

Allie on time

'Allie! ALLIE!' shouted Mum from the kitchen. 'Are you still in bed? Jacqueline's washed and had her breakfast! Hurry up!'

The door banged and Jacqueline came in. Allie screwed up her eyes and burrowed deep under the duvet. It was dark and warm. It was her own little cave. I wish I could sleep here all winter, like a bear,

Allie thought. But suddenly a cold swish of air hit Allie. Jacqueline had pulled the duvet off and thrown it on the floor.

'Get up, Allie! I'm going to be late because of you.'

Allie rolled herself up into a tight ball. Jacqueline threw a pillow at Allie's head. Then Mum came in, and Allie sat up.

'Go and wash NOW,' said Mum. She had her nurse's uniform on. 'Hurry up, Allie, or you won't get any breakfast. I can't be late for work today.'

'And I can't be late for school today,' said Jacqueline.

Allie picked up her clothes from the chair. 'Jacqueline threw my new duvet on the floor,' she said to Mum.

'I'm not surprised,' said Mum. 'If you aren't ready in five minutes you won't get any money for crisps today.'

In the bathroom Allie squeezed the

toothpaste. A long red-and-white striped curl of paste came out. It missed Allie's toothbrush and dropped on the floor. Allie squeezed the tube again. The toothpaste was like paint.

I could make a toothpaste picture, thought Allie. She started to squeeze out enough toothpaste for a red-and-white striped helter-skelter. But just then someone thumped on the bathroom door.

'Allie! ALLIE!'

Allie and Jacqueline had to run to school.

'I hate you,' panted Jacqueline. 'You always make me late. Why can't you ever be on time?'

15

Every day Allie had to meet Jacqueline in the playground so they could walk home together. Allie never had any time to stay and play on the wooden boat. If she was late Jacqueline and her friend Yasmin shouted at her. They walked fast with their heads close together, telling each other secrets they wouldn't tell Allie.

'Hurry up, Allie. Why are you so slow?'

When they got home Allie flopped down in front of the TV. But Jacqueline turned it off.

'You've got to tidy our room first. Mum said so. Your stuff is all over my bit of the floor. Hurry up, Allie!'

Allie went sadly to the bedroom.

When Mum came home Allie waited till Jacqueline had gone round to

Yasmin's house. Then she leaned against Mum and said, 'Can you play a game with me?'

'Not now,' said Mum. 'I've got to do the ironing and make packed lunches for tomorrow. But if I hurry, we might get time later.'

'Hurry,' said Allie. 'Hurry, hurry, hurry. That's all I hear. You're always telling me to hurry. Jacqueline's always bossing me and saying I'm slow.'

'Oh dear,' said Mum. 'But I have to go to work, and you have to go to school. We have to be on time.'

'Yes, but not ALL the time,' said Allie. 'I wish all the clocks in the world would disappear.'

The next day Mum came home with a little box in her hand. It was wrapped in shiny red paper. She smiled at Allie and said, 'It's for you.'

'That's not fair,' said Jacqueline.

'You went to the ice rink on Saturday, Allie didn't,' said Mum. 'Open it, Allie.'

Inside the shiny red paper there was a black box. Allie opened it very slowly. Under the lid, snug in a satin lining, there was a watch. It had a red strap and a beautiful yellow face, and it was just the right size for Allie. It showed the time and the date and it had a little alarm.

'Go on, put it on,' said Mum, and Allie put it on. She turned her wrist this way and that way. It was the best watch she had ever seen.

'There,' said Mum, 'I thought that would help you to be on time.'

'The time is six twelve and fifteen seconds,' said Allie.

'Let *me* try it on,' said Jacqueline.

'No, your hand is too big,' said Allie. 'The time now is six twelve and twenty-four seconds. What time shall I set the alarm for, Mum?'

'Oh, seven thirty will be fine,' said Mum.

But Allie secretly set the little alarm for six o'clock. She thought it would be fun to get up early with her watch.

She wore her watch all night and in the morning her alarm went off when it was still dark. Allie got up and tiptoed to Jacqueline's bed. Jacqueline was fast asleep. Allie pulled off Jacqueline's duvet.

'Urgh! Argh! What's happening?' shouted Jacqueline.

'I want to get to school on time,' said Allie. Jacqueline tried to hit her, but Allie jumped out of the way and went to the bathroom.

All day Allie was on time. She was the first to finish breakfast and the first to put her packed lunch in her schoolbag. She ran through the school gates ahead of Jacqueline. After school she was out in the playground like lightning. After a while Yasmin and Jacqueline came out. Jacqueline looked tired.

'Hurry up,' said Allie. 'It's three thirty-eight and sixteen seconds already. If we hurry we can be home by four.'

At home Jacqueline wanted to sit and watch TV with Yasmin.

'No,' said Allie. 'Remember, Mum said

we had to go and buy pizzas from Mrs Patel, and collect her coat from the dry-cleaner. If we hurry we can make tea before Mum gets home. We've got one hour and fifty minutes and thirty-two seconds.'

Jacqueline got up very slowly. Allie was already waiting by the front door.

Mum was late home that night. Ten minutes and forty-two seconds late.

'Where's Jacqueline?' she asked.

'Oh, I don't know,' said Allie, 'but we're having tea in three minutes and thirty seconds, so she'd better hurry up.'

Allie set her alarm for six thirty the next morning. It was very quiet when she woke up. Jacqueline was asleep, and Allie didn't think it was a good idea to pull off the duvet again.

She went into Mum's room and got

into her bed. Mum rolled over and pulled the duvet over her head.

'It's morning,' said Allie. 'Six thirty-seven and twenty-two seconds.'

'Oh, Allie,' said Mum's sleepy voice. 'It's Saturday. Go back to bed.'

'I thought if we got up early we'd have time to do lots of things,' said Allie. 'Six thirty-eight. Eight minutes gone already since I woke up.'

Mum groaned, so Allie went away.

At breakfast Allie said, 'In four minutes and six seconds I'm going out to buy my sweets. Then at nine thirty I'm going to watch my programme. It finishes at ten. I'm going to read my comic for fifteen minutes before we go shopping. We're going shopping at ten fifteen, Jacqueline.'

'Take away her watch, Mum,' begged Jacqueline.

'Hurry up with that toast,' said Allie, 'I want to be on time.'

'I'll kill you,' said Jacqueline, but Allie escaped round the table.

'There's a time for hurrying,' said Mum, 'and a time for not hurrying.'

'How do you know which is which?' asked Allie.

'OK,' said Mum, 'we'll do a chart. Red days are hurrying days. Monday to Friday. Yellow days are no-worry days. That's weekends and holidays.'

'All right,' said Allie.

'I'll make the chart,' said Jacqueline. 'I'm best at drawing.'

'No,' said Mum, 'you both make it. Together.'

Allie and Jacqueline made a beautiful long chart to hang on the back of the kitchen door. Monday to Friday were coloured red. Allie wrote, HURRY BUT DON'T NAG down the side of the red days. Jacqueline coloured Saturday and Sunday bright yellow. Allie and Jacqueline wrote, NO HURRIES, NO WORRIES down the side of the weekend days.

'No hurries, no worries,' said Allie. 'Sounds good.'

'Yeah,' said Jacqueline. 'Listen, Allie, can I wear your watch? Just for a bit? Please?'

'OK,' said Allie.

Jacqueline put on the watch. 'The time is eleven sixteen and twenty-eight seconds,' she said, 'BUT –

'NO HURRIES, NO WORRIES!' shouted Allie and Jacqueline together.

3

Allie, Misha and the secret frog

'Someone new is coming into our class tomorrow,' said Mrs Button. 'Her name is Misha. Allie! Will you stop talking to Lin and listen to me!'

It was Lin talking to Allie, not Allie talking to Lin, but Allie didn't say anything.

'I want *you* especially to listen very carefully, Allie, because I'm choosing you to be Misha's class friend.'

'Oh,' said Allie. Every time a new child came into Allie's class Mrs Button chose a class friend for her, to show the new one where to go at dinner-time, and look after her in the playground.

'Oh,' said Allie again. Mrs Button had never chosen her to be a class friend before.

'Well, you don't sound very pleased, Allie,' said Mrs Button. 'I hope you're going to make Misha feel welcome in our class.' Her long dangly earrings spun and flashed.

'Yes, Mrs Button,' said Allie.

Lin poked Allie's arm and whispered, 'You can't do juggling with me tomorrow. *You've* got to look after little baby Misha!' Lin was teaching Allie how to juggle.

'*I* didn't want to be Misha's class friend!' said Allie. 'Mrs Button made me.'

27

But Lin shrugged. 'Anyway, Jackie-Louise and Bina both want to have juggling lessons, so you'll have to go down to the bottom of the waiting-list.'

Next morning Allie got to school early. Mrs Button was in the classroom, putting pictures on the wall with a staple-gun.

'Oh good, Allie. Nice and early,' said Mrs Button. 'Come and say hello to Misha. Misha! Oh, dear. She was in the book corner a minute ago.'

'Maybe she's run away,' said Allie.

'I don't think so. Oh, here she is!'

Misha was at the drawing table,

behind the easel. She was drawing some catkins Mrs Button had arranged in a glass jar. All Allie could see was Misha's short, shiny hair and her hand moving as she drew. She walked quietly up behind Misha and looked over her shoulder at the drawing. It was really good. Misha's drawing looked just like the real glass jar. There were even little reflections in  it. And Misha's catkins hung down in shivery tassels just like real catkins.

'Wow!' said Allie. 'I wish I could draw like that.'

Misha was going to be the best in the class at drawing, even better than Lin. But Misha put down her pencil and scrunched the paper into a ball.

'Why did you do that?' asked Allie.

'It was all wrong,' said Misha, and she took another bit of paper and started another drawing. Allie watched the way the shape of the jar grew out of the end of Misha's pencil.

'I'm your class friend,' said Allie.

'I know,' said Misha, drawing.

After break it was time for gym, but Misha hadn't got any shorts. Lin giggled to Jackie-Louise, 'Mrs Button'll make her do it in her knickers!' but Mrs Button told the class to wait, and then she took a carrier bag out from behind her desk and gave it to Allie.

'These are plants for the new wildlife garden. Allie, you remember the bed we dug over by the pond last week? These

plants can go in there. They need to be near water.' She gave a trowel to Misha. 'You carry this, Misha.'

'It's not fair!' hissed Lin as Misha and Allie went past. '*I've* got a proper garden at home. I bet you muck it up!' But Misha just smiled as if she thought Lin was funny.

The wildlife garden was all new. Class 6 had dug the pond, and a bit of its plastic liner poked up through the soil. There was bare earth all around, and a few plants with labels on them. Mrs Button said that soon there'd be pond-skaters and butterflies and maybe even a dragonfly on their pond.

'Not much wildlife here,' said Misha, looking round.

'I think it's nice,' said Allie.

'Do you?' Misha gave Allie a big

sparkly smile. 'I bet it's nicer than Lin's garden, anyway! She thinks she's so big, doesn't she?' Allie stared at Misha. How did she dare say that about Lin? Lin was the boss of the whole class. Everyone wanted to be Lin's friend.

Misha knelt down right on the edge of the pond and looked into the water.

'No tadpoles,' she said. 'Why haven't you got tadpoles?'

'I don't know. Where do you get tadpoles from?'

'They have them at the City Farm,' said Misha. 'I saw them last year. Maybe I could get some.'

Allie thought of tadpoles wriggling in the school pond. And then millions of

frogs hopping
all over the
wildlife garden.
Maybe even hopping into the classroom
and jumping on to Mrs Button's desk.

'Can you really get tadpoles?' she
asked Misha.

Misha shrugged. 'I might,' she said.

But next morning Misha came into
school with no tadpoles.

'Did you go? Did you ask?' said Allie.

'It's too early. They said there aren't
any tadpoles yet. Not even any
frogspawn.'

'Oh.' Allie did not know what
frogspawn was, but Lin was listening so
she didn't ask.

After dinner Mrs Button said, 'You
planted those plants nicely, Allie and
Misha. But the soil is very dry. They'll

need lots of water until their roots are strong. I want you to water them every day.'

'Can we go now?' asked Allie.

'Yes, all right. But don't be silly with that outside tap, will you?'

'*I'll* show them,' said Lin in a loud voice. 'I've got an outside tap in my garden at home.'

Mrs Button looked at her. 'I think Allie and Misha can do the job, Lin,' she said.

There was a heavy watering-can by the outside tap. Misha put it under the tap, and Allie turned the tap on. The pipe groaned and gurgled, then a spurt of water rushed out and hit the inside of the watering-

34

can. Something shot up into the air like an explosion.

'Yow!' screamed Misha. 'What was that?'

'Look! Look!' Allie pointed. It was a frog, a frog the size of Allie's fist. It crouched down on the concrete under the tap. Its throat went in and out fast.

'It must have been living in the watering-can,' said Allie.

'Hey, listen, it can go in the pond,' said Misha. Allie and Misha looked at each other.

'Don't tell Lin,' said Misha. 'Frogs don't like being bossed around.'

Allie laughed.

She crouched down to look at the frog. The round shiny eyes in the top of its head stared back at her, hard.

'Quick, have you got a bit of paper?' asked Misha, but Allie hadn't.

'I want to do a drawing of it,' said Misha. But just then the frog jumped high in the air. Its body stretched right out. Then it landed on its back legs in the shade under a bush. Its legs snapped shut. They could hardly see it.

'It's frightened of us,' said Allie.

'Stupid thing, we're not going to hurt it,' said Misha, and she curled her fingers and wriggled them at the frog. But it wouldn't come to her.

'We'd better go in,' said Allie, 'or Mrs Button will come out.'

The next day the frog was there again. Allie and Misha slopped lots of water over the plants. The frog was half under a stone.

'Why doesn't he go in the pond?'

asked Misha.

'We could put him in,' suggested Allie.

'I want to draw him first,' said Misha, and she took out a folded-up piece of paper and a black felt-tip. Misha began to draw. The lines flowed on to the paper like magic. There was the stone and the folded-up frog with its shiny eyes. Suddenly the frog gave an enormous leap. Over the pond, over a heap of stones and into the bottom of a drainpipe. But Misha's drawing was finished.

'He'll be here again tomorrow,' said Allie.

But the next day the frog wasn't there.

Allie wriggled under the bushes and searched the damp earth. Misha pushed a stick up the drainpipe in case the frog was stuck. They looked everywhere but there was no frog.

'I wish I had a photo of him,' said Allie.

'I've got my drawing,' said Misha. 'I could do a copy for you in the school office if you want. It only costs five pence.'

'Yes, please!' said Allie. Misha's drawing was much better than a photo.

'Hey!' shouted Misha. 'Hey, look, Allie! Look what's in the pond!'

Allie rushed to the edge of the water. The pond was full of white jelly with black points in it. It was puffed up like a pillow in the water.

'Frogspawn!' said Misha. 'That frog

must have left it.'

Allie poked her finger into the water and touched the edge of the frogspawn. It slithered away.

'Each of those black dots will turn into a frog,' said Misha.

'Wow,' said Allie. Then she thought of Lin. If Lin found out about the frogs she would spoil it. She would tell everyone. 'Let's keep it a secret.'

'OK,' said Misha. 'Listen, Allie, can you stop being my class friend?'

Allie stared at the frogspawn. It wobbled and Allie blinked.

'Can you be my real friend instead?' asked Misha.

Allie looked up. Misha smiled her big sparkly smile again and Allie smiled back.

'Yes,' she said. 'Yes, of course I can!'

4

Allie and Misha make money

Jacqueline shook coins out of her money-box and counted them into piles. 'How much have you got?' asked Allie.

'Nine pounds sixty – nine pounds eighty – nine pounds ninety-five. Nearly enough,' said Jacqueline.

'Enough for what?'

'My Mother's Day present for Mum. I'm getting her silver earrings.'

Allie knelt up on her bed. 'Mother's Day!' she said. 'When's that?'

'Two weeks on Sunday,' said Jacqueline.

'Oh no!' said Allie. 'I haven't got any money.'

'What about your birthday money?'

'It's all gone. Please, Jacqueline, *please* lend me a pound. *Please.* I can get Mum some flowers with a pound. You don't need all that money for her present.'

'Yes I do. The earrings cost twelve pounds ninety-nine,' said Jacqueline in a proud voice.

'Twelve pounds ninety-nine!' Allie fell back on her bed.

'This is going to be the best Mother's Day present Mum's ever had,' said Jacqueline. Allie watched her pour her money back into her money-box and turn the little key.

'I'm going round to Misha's,' Allie said. She banged the front door shut and ran along the street. Misha lived round the corner and down the next street.

Misha was playing with her baby sister, Vivi. Vivi was lying on her back and laughing every time Misha tickled her tummy. Allie wished she had a baby sister instead of Jacqueline.

'Misha,' she said, 'what're you getting your mum for Mother's Day?'

'Mother's Day!' said Misha. She stopped tickling Vivi and sat still, staring at Allie. 'When's Mother's Day?'

'Two weeks on Sunday. Jacqueline's getting Mum earrings that cost twelve pounds ninety-nine, and I haven't got any money.'

'Me neither,' said Misha. 'Maybe we

could earn some.'

But Allie had tried that before. She wasn't old enough for a paper round. She wasn't old enough to wash cars. She was too young for everything.

'There must be something,' said Misha. 'Something we're good at.'

Vivi cried and Misha swung her up high and made her laugh. Allie thought hard about what she was good at. Quite good at running but not good enough to win a prize. She could cook. She could do beans on toast and sausages and mash.

'Misha! We could have a stall and sell cakes and biscuits and stuff!'

'Can you make cakes?'

'No, but it's easy. I've seen Mum make them loads of times.'

'But you have to buy eggs and sugar and things first, and we haven't got any money,' said Misha. 'Anyway, where could we sell them?'

Suddenly Allie had a brilliant idea. 'I know! We could sell them at Hurley Park Street Fair!'

Hurley Park Street Fair happened every spring. There were stalls up and down Hurley Road. Anyone could have a stall as long as they gave half their money to the Park Fund.

'Yeah!' said Misha. 'Hurley Park Street Fair! But not cakes. We haven't got enough money to make cakes. What else can we sell? What else are we good at?'

'Oh!' said Allie. 'Listen, Misha. Your drawings! We can sell your drawings!'

Misha flushed. 'No one would buy them,' she said.

'They would! They would! You could

do pictures of people.'

'Portraits, you mean?' asked Misha.

'Yeah – they could sit on a stool and you could draw them. We could charge twenty pence each. And we can have frames. I'll make frames out of card, like Mrs Button does for our paintings at school. She'll show me how. Hey, watch Vivi, she's eating your mum's shoe.'

Misha grabbed Vivi and Vivi screamed with rage.

'Do you really think I'm good enough?' asked Allie.

'Course you are! You're brilliant!'

Misha's eyes sparkled.

Hurley Park Street Fair was the day before Mother's Day. It took ages to make the frames. Mrs Button let them have two big sheets of red card and they promised to give her the money after the fair. She showed them how to cut out strips of red card, staple them into a rectangle and then stick a back on the frame. The backs were made out of cornflake packets. When the frames were finished you could slide the drawing in at the side. Every day Allie and Misha made frames.

'What are you two doing up there?' asked Misha's mum.

'Nothing. It's a secret.'

The day of the fair came. Allie and Misha brought three folding chairs. They stuck drawings on their stall with Sellotape so people could see how good Misha's drawings were. Misha had a big clipboard to lean on, and a pile of

drawing paper. She had pencils and charcoal and two pens. Her dad helped to carry all the stuff up to Hurley Road.

Everywhere people were setting up

stalls. Food stalls and clothes stalls and face-painting stalls and ice-cream stalls. Allie sat behind the table with the money tin. Misha sat on one of the folding chairs. The other chair was empty, waiting for the first customer.

'OK, girls, I'll be over there on the white elephant stall,' said Misha's dad. 'Shout if you need me.'

Soon people started to come. They

stopped and peered at Misha's drawings on the table.

'Ooh, that's nice. I like that one,' said a woman. 'How much?'

'It's not for sale,' said Misha. 'Do you want me to do your portrait?'

'Oh no,' said the woman, and she went on to another stall.

Then three teenagers came along. They pushed each other and shouted. They stopped at Allie and Misha's stall.

'Hey, look at this! She'll do your portrait for you,' said one of them.

'Give it to your girlfriend, Baz,' said the biggest one, and they all laughed.

'They're only little kids. It'll be rubbish.'

But the biggest boy was leaning over the table and looking at the drawings.

'They're not bad. How much is it?'

'Twenty pence,' said Allie. 'You can

give it to your mum for Mother's Day.'

'Mother's Day, is it? All right, go on then,' and he sat down on the folding chair.

Misha picked up a pencil and began to draw with long, sure strokes. The other two boys looked over her shoulder, but Misha didn't care. All she cared about was her drawing. When it was finished she unclipped it and gave it to the boy who was sitting on the chair. He looked at it for a long time, then slowly he smiled.

'This kid's good,' he said.

'We'll put it in a frame for you,' said Allie, and she slid the drawing into one of the red frames.

'How much is the frame?' asked the teenager.

'Nothing,' said Allie.

'You could charge fifty pence for that drawing with the frame,' said the boy.

All the teenagers had their portraits done. When they had gone Allie jumped up and changed *'Portraits 20p'* to *'Portraits 50p with frame'*. Suddenly there was a queue of people waiting for their portraits.

Allie took the money, Misha drew, then Allie put the drawings into their frames. Misha drew and drew and drew. As soon as one person got off the folding chair, another sat down. The money tin was getting heavier and heavier. Misha went on and on.

She's like a drawing machine, thought

Allie. They were running out of frames.

Suddenly it was all over. People were packing up and the crowds had gone. Misha stood up and stretched.

'How much have we got?' she asked. Allie was still counting. Slowly she counted all their money back into the tin.

'Twenty-three pounds twenty pence!' she said.

'We've got to give half to the Park Fund, and a pound to Mrs Button. How much is left?'

Allie wrote down the sum and worked it out. 'I think we get five pounds thirty each,' she said.

'Fantastic!' said Misha. Then she looked at Allie and asked, 'Do you want me to draw you?'

'OK,' said Allie, and Misha drew.

Allie put the portrait carefully into the frame and took it home with the money. She bought a beautiful jasmine plant for Mum, and a card with a baby hedgehog on it.

On Mother's Day morning she and Jacqueline proudly gave Mum her presents. Mum put the earrings on right away, and sniffed the sweet jasmine. She read her cards and Jacqueline went off to make Mum a cup of tea. Then Mum saw the red frame. 'What's this?'

'Turn it over and look,' said Allie.

Mum turned it over. She saw the drawing of Allie. 'Oh!' she said. 'Oh, how beautiful! Oh, Allie!' and her face went all crumply.

'You do like it, don't you?' asked Allie.

'It's wonderful,' said Mum.

'Good,' said Allie. 'But that jasmine cost a lot of money.'

Mum's face went all crumply again, but this time it was because she was laughing.

Later on Allie saw Misha. 'It's funny,' she said, 'I think she liked your drawing best. So we didn't need all that money.'

'My mum was just the same,' Misha said. 'I gave her a drawing of Vivi and she said it was the best Mother's Day present she'd ever had!'

If you enjoyed this
MAMMOTH STORYBOOK

look out for:

Little Mouse Grandma

Julia Jarman
Illustrated by Alex de Wolf
~
Matthew's grandmother has an
incredible secret!

When nobody's about – except Matthew, of
course – she turns into a mouse!
So Matthew loves it when Grandma
looks after him.
But then Matthew is given a tiny, soft,
golden-brown kitten –
and the trouble begins . . .

If you enjoyed this
MAMMOTH STORYBOOK
look out for:

Blair the Winner!

Theresa Breslin
Illustrated by *Ken Cox*

~

It's not fair being in the middle,
like Blair.

Little baby Willis is a pest.
Big sister Melissa thinks Blair's the pest.
And all the family never stop nagging!

But it's Blair who saves the day
on a camping trip that goes wrong . . .

If you enjoyed this
MAMMOTH STORYBOOK

look out for:

Tricky Tricky Twins

Kate Elizabeth Ernest
Illustrated by David Mitchell
~
Cudjoe and Jonah are the naughtiest
twins in Jamaica!

They upset goody-goody Clara . . .
They make fun of posh Lydia and Roger . . .
And they can't help teasing poor
Granny Elvira!

Is Grandpa Gilbert brave enough to put them
in their place at last?

A Selected List of Fiction from Mammoth

While every effort is made to keep prices low, it is sometimes necessary to increase prices at short notice . Mandarin Paperbacks reserves the right to show new retail prices on covers which may differ from those previously advertised in the text or elsewhere.

The prices shown below were correct at the time of going to press.

☐	7497 2646 6	**The Face at the Window**	Vivien Alcock	£3.99
☐	7497 2067 0	**The Parsley Parcel**	Elizabeth Arnold	£3.99
☐	7497 2388 2	**Whispers in the Graveyard**	Theresa Breslin	£3.99
☐	7497 1794 7	**Born of the Sun**	Gillian Cross	£3.99
☐	7497 1066 7	**The Animals of Farthing Wood**	Colin Dann	£3.99
☐	7497 1823 4	**White Peak Farm**	Berlie Doherty	£3.50
☐	7497 0184 6	**The Summer House Loon**	Anne Fine	£3.99
☐	7497 0962 6	**The Away Team**	Michael Hardcastle	£2.99
☐	7497 0136 6	**I Am David**	Anne Holm	£3.99
☐	7497 1664 9	**Hiding Out**	Elizabeth Laird	£4.50
☐	7497 0791 7	**The Ghost of Thomas Kempe**	Penelope Lively	£3.99
☐	7497 2644 X	**The Voices of Silence**	Bel Mooney	£3.99
☐	7497 1754 8	**The War of Jenkins' Ear**	Michael Morpurgo	£3.99
☐	7497 0831 X	**The Snow Spider**	Jenny Nimmo	£3.99
☐	7497 0656 2	**Journey of 1000 Miles**	Ian Strachan	£3.99
☐	7497 2734 9	**Panther in Argyll**	Lisa Tuttle	£3.99
☐	7497 0796 8	**Kingdom by the Sea**	Robert Westall	£3.99

All these books are available at your bookshop or newsagent, or can be ordered direct from the address below. Just tick the titles you want and fill in the form below.

Cash Sales Department, PO Box 5, Rushden, Northants NN10 6YX.
Fax: 01933 414047 : Phone: 01933 414000.

Please send cheque, payable to 'Reed Book Services Ltd.', or postal order for purchase price quoted and allow the following for postage and packing:

£1.00 for the first book, 50p for the second; **FREE POSTAGE AND PACKING FOR THREE BOOKS OR MORE PER ORDER.**

NAME (Block letters)..

ADDRESS...

....

☐ I enclose my remittance for...........................

☐ I wish to pay by Access/Visa Card Number

Expiry Date

Signature . . . .

Please quote our reference: MAND